Copycat

Iris Howden

Published in association with
The Basic Skills Agency

Acknowledgements
Cover: Stephanie Hawken
Illustrations: Maureen Carter

Orders; please contact Bookpoint Ltd, 39 Milton Park, Abingdon, Oxon OX14
4TD. Telephone: (44) 01235 400414, Fax: (44) 01235 400454. Lines are open
from 9.00–6.00, Monday to Saturday, with a 24 hour message answering service.
Email address: orders@bookpoint.co.uk

British Library Cataloguing in Publication Data
A catalogue record for this title is available from the British Library

ISBN 0 340 77607 2

First published 2000
Impression number 10 9 8 7 6 5 4 3 2 1
Year   2005 2004 2003 2002 2001 2000

Typeset by GreenGate Publishing Services, Tonbridge, Kent.
Printed in Great Britain for Hodder and Stoughton Educational, a division of
Hodder Headline Plc, 338 Euston Road, London NW1 3BH, by Atheneum
Press, Gateshead, Tyne & Wear

Copycat

Contents

1

A New Sister

I was 12 when my mum got married again.
Her new husband's name was Jeff.
Jeff had a daughter too.
Her name was Mandy.
She was the same age as me.
After the wedding, Jeff and Mandy
moved into our house.
We were to be a family.

'Aren't you lucky, Emma,' my Aunty Pam said,
'having a ready-made sister.'
I wasn't so sure.
Mum and I were used to living alone.
She and my dad split up years ago.
He lives in Australia now.
He has a new wife and two small children.

Mandy's mother had died when she was little.
So she was very close to her dad.
It was going to take time for us all
to get used to each other.
At first I think we tried too hard.
We were too polite.
We weren't at ease with each other,
like a real family.

Mum found it hard to tell Mandy off.
I would be in trouble
if I left my things lying around.
Mum would pick Mandy's up
and put them away.
If I was late home and hadn't phoned
to let Mum know, she shouted at me.
Mandy could come and go as she pleased.
'I expect you forgot,' Mum said to her once.

I didn't have a problem with Jeff.
He was a nice man. I liked him
but I thought he was too soft with Mandy.
She could always get round him.
If she wanted something, she'd ask Jeff.
'Please Daddy,' she'd say,
and roll her big blue eyes.
'Please, Daddy.' She used this silly baby voice.
It made me want to throw up.

Right from the start
she wanted everything I had.
Mum and Aunty Pam always bought
us the same presents.

If a friend gave me something different
Mandy had to have one. Whatever it was:
a toy, a book, even a hairslide.
If I chose a blue T-shirt,
Mandy wanted a blue one too.
If I had my hair cut a new way,
Mandy had the same style.
She even copied my handwriting.
'I like the way you do your capitals,' she said.
'Show me how to do them, Emma.'

'You should be pleased Mandy
wants to be like you,' Aunty Pam said.
'It shows she really likes you.'
But I wasn't happy about it.
She was such a copycat.

I was glad she wasn't in my class at school.
Even there, she copied me.
We had to have the same jackets.
The same sort of games shoes.
The same lunch boxes.
We even had the same sandwiches.

I tried to find something she didn't like.
'I'll have sardines in my sandwich,' I told Mum.
Mum was surprised.
She knew I didn't like sardines very much.
'Good idea,' Mandy said. 'I'll have the same.'
She was a real pain.

As we got older I tried to shake her off.
I chose different subjects for GCSE.
I planned to go to college afterwards.
I was taking languages, French and German,
at 'A' level. I wanted to work abroad.

I was hoping Mandy wouldn't go to college
but I was out of luck.
Our local college ran all sorts of courses.
Mandy soon found one that suited her.
'Beauty Therapy,' she told me.
'That's what I'll do.
I'm not as brainy as you are, Emma.
You don't need as many GCSEs for that,
but we'll be together at college.
Won't that be nice?'

2

Growing Up

After five years I didn't like Mandy any better.
I tried not to show it at home.
Mum and Jeff were happy together.
I didn't want to spoil things for them.
Besides, what could I say?
To other people, Mandy seemed really nice.
Only I knew what she was really like.
How she always got her own way.

If we did the washing up together,
she'd grab the tea towel.
'You wash, I'll dry,' she'd say.
This meant I had to scrub all the greasy pans.
If we helped Mum with the ironing
Mandy did all the flat things.
She left the shirts for me.
She'd go into my room and borrow
anything of mine that took her fancy.
'Oh sorry, Emma,' she'd say.
'I didn't think you'd mind.
I'd let you borrow my things.'
This made me look really mean.

I took to going round to Aunty Pam's.
She was the only one I could talk to.
Aunty Pam had two cats.
Mandy didn't like cats.
Their fur made her sneeze.
'Sisters don't always get on,' Aunty Pam said.
'Your mum and I used to fight
all the time when we were young.'
'We don't fight,' I said.
'I just don't like her.'

By now we were both coming up to 17.
Mandy was very pretty.
She was small and slim with blonde hair.
She still had those big blue eyes.
That cute little nose.
She made me feel big and clumsy.
Next to Mandy I looked plain.
'You're just as pretty,' Aunty Pam told me.
'You're just a different type.
I do wish you two got along better.
You could have a lot of fun together.'

Mandy had friends of her own.
But she always wanted to join mine.
To do what we were doing.
'Your step-sister's sweet,' my friends would say.
Mandy could turn on the charm
when she wanted.

There was this boy I really liked.
His name was Rick.
We went out together a few times.
We were getting on really well –
until he met Mandy.
She went out of her way to steal him.
She hung on his every word.
Laughed at his jokes.
Sat close to him on the settee.

After a week or two he stopped calling me.
He made excuses if we met in college.
'I've been busy,' he said. 'I'll ring you.'
I knew he was lying.
He was seeing Mandy.
My friend Ginny had seen them together
at the cinema.
I was really hurt.

I made up my mind to speak to Mandy.
'Oh Emma,' she said. 'I didn't know things
were serious between you and Rick.
I thought you were just friends,
or I'd never have gone out with him.'

She only went out with him
a couple of times after that.
It was taking him away from me
that she liked.
Just as, when we were young,
she'd wanted my comic or my new CD.

3

Driving Lessons

When we were 18 Jeff said he would pay
for driving lessons for us both.
It was his birthday present to us.
I was really pleased.
Mandy wasn't so keen.
'I'm not sure I could ever learn to drive,'
she told Jeff.
'Nonsense,' Jeff said. 'Anyone can learn.
Driving's a skill you need nowadays.
What do you think, Emma?'
'I'd love to learn,' I said. 'Thanks Jeff.'

'Oh well, if Emma's going to learn,
I might as well,' Mandy said.
Just as I knew she would.

We got the forms for a licence.
'You have to take a written test
as well now,' Jeff said.
'Make sure you learn the Highway Code.'
'I'll never remember all this,' Mandy said.
'You'll have to help me, Emma.
You're better at this kind of thing.'
She could never do anything for herself.

The lessons were booked.
I was really looking forward to them.
The driving instructor came to pick us up.
He was a fat, middle-aged man.
His name was Mr Sanders.
It was my turn first.
'Just relax,' Mr Sanders told me.
'We'll run through the basics.
Then I'll take you out on the road.'

That first hour was a nightmare.
I couldn't do a thing right.
I crunched the gears.
I forgot to look in the mirror.
I let the handbrake slip.
Mr Sanders was very patient.
'Don't worry about it, Emma,' he said.
'Everyone's nervous at first.
You'll soon get the hang of it.'

When Mandy's hour was over
she ran into the house.
She had a big smile on her face.
'Wasn't it great?' she said.
'I had a really good lesson.
Mr Sanders said I did really well.
I'm going to love driving.'

I thought this was just chance.
That I would soon pick it up.
But that wasn't the case.
The weeks went by.
I didn't seem to make any progress.

Mandy, on the other hand, was soon
driving quite well.
Even I could see the difference.
She drove away smoothly from the kerb.
I never set off without making
the car stall.

Soon Mandy was doing three-point turns.
She could reverse neatly round corners.
Mr Sanders took her along the busy high street.
He took me in quiet lanes.
If I tried something like a three-point turn
it was a disaster.
The car went all over the place.
'I don't think you're quite ready for that yet,'
Mr Sanders told me.
'By the way,' he said. 'I shall be away
for a few weeks.
I'm going to visit my brother in Canada.
My son, Danny, will take your lessons.
Maybe you'll do better with him.'

But I didn't.
Danny was not a bit like his dad.
To start with he had film star looks:
wavy hair, blue eyes, perfect white teeth.
His voice was deep and husky.
Danny had loads of charm.
I fell for him the moment I saw him.
It was hard to keep my mind on the lesson.
So I was even worse than usual.

Danny was very nice about it.
'Don't worry about it,' he said.
He put his strong brown arm
round my shoulder.
'Your neck muscles are very tense,' he said.
'You need to relax a bit.
Try to enjoy driving. Copy your sister Mandy.'

This didn't make me feel any better.
I couldn't believe Mandy was so good
at driving while I was so bad.
I was usually quick to learn.
Now I looked like an idiot.
While Mandy made it look so easy.

Within weeks she was ready to take her test.
I hadn't a hope of taking mine.
She passed first time.
To make matters worse she told me
she was going out to celebrate – with Danny.
'Danny's asked me out,' Mandy said.
'He said he's wanted to for ages
but he couldn't while he was my teacher.
He waited till I'd got my licence.
Wasn't that sweet?'

'Great,' I said. I had to grit my teeth
to answer her.
Now I was the one to feel jealous.
To want what my sister had.
I had really wanted to learn to drive.
To get my licence.
I'd had such a crush on Danny.
It had never struck me that
he was keen on Mandy.
How could I have been such a fool?
'It's not fair!' I told Aunty Pam.
I knew I sounded just like Mandy had
– when we were 12 years old.

I couldn't face Danny again.
I waited till Mr Sanders came back
from Canada.
Then I went on with my lessons.
All at once, I began to improve.
Driving became easier.
Jeff took me out for extra practice.
At last, I was ready to take my test.
I passed first time.

4

Moving On

It was our last term at college.
We began to apply for jobs.
I wanted to work abroad so I could
use my languages.
I started to look in the papers
that had adverts for jobs in Europe.

I had always wanted to work abroad.
Now I had another reason for going.
I wanted to get far away
from Mandy and Danny.

They were an item by this time.
He was often round at our house.
I couldn't bear to see them together.

Mandy got a job in a local beauty salon.
It wasn't well paid but she wanted
to stay in our home town.
So she could be near Danny.
Then it was my turn.
I got an interview for a job.
The interview was held in London.

The job was with a big company.
The company's main office was in Brussels.
It had branches in other cities in Europe.
If I got the job
I would have the chance to travel.
To see different parts of Europe.
It was exactly what I wanted.

The interview went well.
A few days later I got a letter telling me
I had got the job.
I was to start on 1 September.

The weeks passed quickly.
I had to buy new clothes.
Sort out what I would need for Brussels.
Say goodbye to everyone.

Mum and Jeff laid on a party for me.
Aunty Pam was there.
All my friends from college came.
Mandy asked Danny of course.
I tried to stay out of his way
but he seemed keen to talk to me.
He followed me into the kitchen.

Then he came up to me.
He put his arm round my waist.
'How about a goodbye kiss,' he said.
I turned my head away.
'I've always liked you, Emma,' he said.
'You've got style.'
He tried to kiss me again.

For a minute I was tempted.
Danny was very attractive.
I wanted to kiss him.
Part of me wanted to pay Mandy back
for stealing Rick that time.
I'd show her I could take her boyfriend too.

Danny tried again.
He wouldn't take no for an answer.
He grabbed hold of my arms.
This was a side of him I hadn't seen before.
I didn't much like it.
He and Mandy were going steady.
Why was he trying to kiss me?
In the end I had to be quite rude.
'Get lost,' I said, and pushed him away.

I wondered if I should warn Mandy.
Tell her what her boyfriend was really like.
In the end I thought better of it.
It was a party after all.
Maybe Danny had drunk too much wine.
Besides, I was going away.
I didn't want to cause trouble.

Once I got to Brussels,
I put Danny out of my mind.
There was so much to do.
I found rooms in a house in the city.
My landlady, Madame Delain, was a widow.
She seemed to take to me.
She treated me like a daughter.
I soon settled into my new home.

Starting work was really exciting.
There were so many people to meet.
So many things to learn.
There was a big city to explore.
I didn't have time to be homesick.

Then Mum wrote to me.
Her letter gave me a shock.
She told me Mandy and Danny
were getting engaged.
Jeff wasn't too happy about it, she said.
He thought Mandy was too young
but Mandy had talked him round.

I had to smile at that bit.
She asked if I could get home
for the engagement party.

I wrote back and made excuses.
I couldn't have any time off, I said.
I was too new to the job.
I wasn't sure I would even make it
back to England for Christmas.
I would have to let them know.
The fact was, I didn't try.
I wanted to keep my distance.

Mum sent me some photos.
Pictures of the happy couple arm in arm,
smiling like crazy.
Mandy showing off her ring.
I stuffed them at the back of a drawer.

5

Friends

I didn't go home for six months.
Mum rang me every week.
She gave me all the news.
One day she told me there was to be
another party. It was for Jeff's birthday.
He would be 50 in March.
'He'd love you to be there,' Mum said.
'Jeff misses you, Emma. We all do.
Please try and make it for his sake.'

I couldn't very well refuse.
I liked Jeff a lot.
He'd been very good to me.
Just like a real father.
I often wished I had called him Dad.
Mandy had begun to call my mother 'Mum'
when they moved into our house.

I asked for some time off
and flew back to England.
My home town seemed very small after Brussels.
Our house looked much the same.
It felt strange to be back in my old room.

I unpacked and went downstairs.
Jeff came home from work.
He was really pleased to see me.
He gave me a hug.
'Emma, you look so grown-up,'
he said, 'and very smart.
I'm so glad you've come home.'

Mum set the table for three.
'Where's Mandy?' I asked her.
We were in the kitchen dishing up the meal.
Mum shut the kitchen door.
She spoke quietly so Jeff couldn't hear.
'Mandy's working late tonight,' she said.
'By the way, she's broken off her engagement
to Danny. I don't know why.
She's very upset.
She won't talk to us about it.
Maybe she'll tell you.'

When Mandy came home she said hello.
Then she went straight to bed.
She looked very tired.
She had black circles under her eyes –
as if she hadn't slept much lately.
The next day Mum and Jeff went out.
They had to do some shopping for the party.

Mandy sat in the kitchen in her dressing gown.
I made a pot of tea and some toast.
I asked Mandy if she wanted some.
She shook her head.

'I don't want anything, thanks, Emma.'
She sat there for ages not speaking.
I didn't know what to say.
I chatted about Brussels.
Told her about my new job.
About the people in the office.
Mandy didn't seem to be listening.

Suddenly she said, 'The engagement's off.
Danny was seeing someone else.
A girl he was teaching to drive.'
'I'm sorry,' I said. I wasn't too surprised.
I had a good idea what Danny was like.
I knew I'd had a lucky escape.
'She wasn't the first,' Mandy went on.
'There were others as well.'

Then she burst into tears.
I felt really sorry for her.
I went across and put my arm round her.
'Don't cry, Mandy,' I said.
'You're better off without him.'
I passed her a tissue.

'You don't understand,' she said.
'He's taken all my money.
He talked me into having a joint account.
We were saving up for the wedding.
I put all my spare cash into it.

I went to the bank the other day to check
how much was in the account.
There was nothing left.
Danny had drawn out all the money.
I haven't even got enough to buy
a decent present for Dad's birthday.
That's why I was doing overtime.
I daren't tell Dad what Danny's done.
He didn't want us to get engaged
in the first place.'

'Don't worry about it now,' I said.
'Leave it until after the party.
I haven't bought my present yet.
Let's go into town today and buy
something special from both of us.
You can pay me back any time.'

Mandy cheered up at this.
We had a good day shopping.
We chose a really nice gift for Jeff.
I wrote on the card:
To Dad from both your daughters,
Love from Mandy and Emma.

'That's a nice message,' Mandy said.
'I feel like we really are sisters now.
You know, Emma, I was so scared,
moving into your house when I was a kid.
Your Mum made me feel welcome
but I never felt you liked me.

'You were always so clever, so confident.
I tried hard to be like you.
I was never very good at anything.
Until we learned to drive, that is.
That seemed to come easily.
It was the first time I'd ever been better
than you at anything.'

I felt ashamed of myself.
I knew I hadn't been fair to Mandy
when we were kids.
I hadn't given her a chance.
Driving was the only thing
I had ever found hard to do.
It had made me feel really stupid.
Poor Mandy must have felt like that quite often.

Suddenly I wanted to make it up to her.
'You'll have to come over and stay with me
in Brussels,' I said.
'See all the sights.'
'That would be great,' Mandy said.
'I love your suit by the way.
Did you get it over there?
I'd like one in that style.'

She went on, 'Maybe I could get a job
in a beauty salon there.
What do you think?'

She sounded much more like her old self.
A real copycat.

'I'm not sure about that,' I said.
'Come for a visit first.
See how you like it.'
I wanted to take things slowly.
If we were going to be sisters,
we had to learn to be friends.